Arctic Shadows: A Lenin Aslanov Story Book 1: The Finnish Incursion

Arctic Shadows: A Lenin Aslanov Story, Volume 1

Maxwell Hoffman

Published by Maxwell Hoffman, 2024.

ARCTIC SHADOWS: A LENIN ASLANOV STORY BOOK 1: THE FINNISH INCURSION

First edition. November 8, 2024.

ISBN: 979-8227397652

Written by Maxwell Hoffman.

Also by Maxwell Hoffman

Acorn Man Savior of the Forest
Acorn Man Savior of the Forest

Arctic Shadows: A Lenin Aslanov Story
Arctic Shadows: A Lenin Aslanov Story Book 1: The Finnish Incursion

Baron Floofnose: A Capybara's Quest
Baron Floofnose: A Capybara's Quest Omnibus Trilogy

Benny Dubious Playbook Scheme Series 3
Benny Dubious Playbook Scheme Trouble in Georgia Book 2: "Moshie's" Fall
Benny Dubious Playbook Scheme Trouble in Georgia Book 3: Hugo's Revelation

Frozen Dawn: A Neanderthal's Redemption
Frozen Dawn: A Neanderthal's Redemption Omnibus Trilogy

Ivan Zhuk: Zhuk's Gambit
Ivan Zhuk: Zhuk's Gambit Book 1 Mental Agony
Ivan Zhuk: Zhuk's Gambit Book 2 The MMA Fighter
Ivan Zhuk: Zhuk's Gambit Book 3 Ivan's Freedom

Knox Sovereign: The Juche Wars
Knox Sovereign: The Juche Wars Book 1 Unmasking Knox Sovereign
Knox Sovereign: The Juche Wars Book 2 A Daring Rescue
Knox Sovereign: The Juche Wars Book 3: Fall of Colonel Rex MacManners

Misadventures of Wolfgang Wirrarr
Misadventures of Wolfgang Wirrarr Omnibus Trilogy

Rowan Sunfire Frosty Fugitive Series
Rowan Sunfire Frosty Fugitive Book 3 Defense of Vos Tower
Rowan Sunfire Frosty Fugitive Omnibus Trilogy

Wiccan Guardian
Wiccan Guardian Omnibus Trilogy

Watch for more at https://www.instagram.com/vader7800/.

Table of Contents

ARCTIC SHADOWS: A LENIN ASLANOV STORY BOOK 1
THE FINNISH INCURSION
by
Maxwell Hoffman

Part One

Prologue

<u>**Sometime in Early 2022**</u>

#

Lenin Aslanov had always hated working for his abusive older brother Dmitry Alsanov. Dmitry was a high-ranking FSB official running his own company known as the Iron Curtain Security. It was their task to ensure they could see any potential weakness with Russia's border with Finland. Things took a turn for the worse when the war in Ukraine broke out, and Lenin hated the idea of following his brother's marching orders. Dmitry was giving his marching orders in his usual tent to his brother.

#

"Listen Lenin, it would be nice if you can figure out if Finland's border has gotten weak since the pandemic" said Dmitry.

#

"But what about the virus?" asked Lenin.

#

"You'll be wearing a mask, so you should be fine" said Dmitry.

#

Dmitry knew his younger brother Lenin was lazy at his job which was the reason for Dmitry's headstrong approach. Lenin sighed, he hated being at the Iron Curtain Security camp. It was so boring and out of the way. He strolled out of the tent after Dmitry gave his instructions. He headed off on his scouting mission towards Finland's border with Russia unsure what to expect.

#

<u>**New Pawns**</u>

#

While Lenin was away, a Russian soldier appeared with some urgent news.

#

"Sir, a shipment of refugees have arrived" said the soldier.

#

The soldier was unsure what to make, they didn't know if they were going to purposely cause a humanitarian crisis with Finland's border as a way to make Russia look innocent.

\#

"Where are the refugees from?" asked Dmitry.

\#

"They're mostly rejects from the Palestinian branch of the Oasis Defense" continued the soldier.

\#

"Let me take a look at them" said Dmitry as he got up.

\#

Dmitry soon strolled out of his tent and the soldier escorted him to where the truck loaded them off. Dmitry could tell some of them could be used for scouting purposes. They had failed the most basic training for the Palestinian cause and were all considered as rejects. Among those rejects included Salem Barid who was so timid and frighten by a mere explosion. He wasn't about to become a martyr at all.

\#

"Everyone state your name, starting with you!" ordered Dmitry.

\#

Salem stood up quite frighten at seeing Dmitry.

\#

"Salem Barid sir!" cried Salem.

\#

Dmitry smiled, he got some sort of sense he was going to use this refugee to be his brother's partner.

\#

<u>Border with Finland</u>

\#

Meanwhile, Lenin continued on his trek towards the Finnish border with Russia. He could see there wasn't that much of a presence despite reports of Finland hoping to join NATO.

\#

"Hmm, doesn't seem to be that many guards" said Lenin as he gazed upon the border with his binoculars in hand.

\#

Lenin could see how poorly guarded this section of the border was, but he'd have to get help. So he decided to trek back, there were only a few Finnish soldiers stationed at the border. As he trekked in the snow, it took Lenin sometime before he could reach the Iron Curtain Security camp. He noticed a truck leaving the camp and didn't think that much until he noticed so many new faces mostly Middle Eastern.

#

"What the heck are they doing here?" asked Lenin.

#

"Orders from the Kremlin, they are going to be free labor workers" laughed one of the soldiers, "you should speak with your brother, he has a special someone to assign to you."

#

Lenin was puzzled by this as he headed over, Dmitry was waiting for him in his tent with Salem being quite frighten.

#

Lenin and Salem

#

Lenin was puzzled - what were Middle Eastern refugees doing here in Russia of all places?

#

"Are you confused to why Salem Barid is here?" asked Dmitry.

#

Lenin had to shake his head signaling a yes.

#

"I have to explain this to you every time" sighed Dmitry, "my bosses in the Kremlin want to create a humanitarian crisis. Since you came back from the Finnish border, what do you have to report on it?"

#

"The portion I arrived is poorly guarded with very few Finnish guards" said Lenin.

#

"Excellent, I would like you to try to lead a group of Palestinian refugees to the Finnish border" continued Dmitry, "I want to see chaos!"

#

Dmitry was being firm with his views on the Kremlin's goal, it was another way for the Kremlin to also get back at Finland for daring to not be part of the Russian Empire even during its Czarist Era. For Salem, this was a frightful moment, he was rejected from the Oasis Defense only to find his way here. Salem soon got up and left with Lenin back to his tent.

#

"Please, I am sorry it's not my intension for this to be like it" said Salem.

#

"My brother can be so bossy" sighed Lenin.

#

Lenin knew things would get bad to worse if he complied with his brother's goals.

Chapter One

<u>Getting to Know Salem</u>

\#

Lenin of all people was curious to know why the Russians were sending Palestinian refugees to do their dirty work for them. He could see that Salem wasn't the typical Palestinian fighter as they walked towards his tent.

\#

"So what brings you to the Russian Federation?" asked Lenin.

\#

"I was sent here because I failed basic training for the Oasis Defense" sighed Salem, "I am not like the other Palestinians. They are so eager to engage in a fight, but not me."

\#

"I can imagine you felt out of place" said Lenin.

\#

Salem nodded, the two soon headed towards Lenin's tent. Lenin pulled up an extra sleeping blanket for Salem.

\#

"I guess you can stay here in my tent for the time being" said Lenin.

\#

"Thank you" said Salem as he soon got ready to go to bed.

\#

Salem couldn't believe that Lenin was the first friendly face he had seen in quite a long time. As he dozed off to sleep, Dmitry continued to inspect the other Palestinian refugees. Mostly military aged men with a few women among the ranks. He could see this would do nicely for the border raid.

\#

<u>Training the Refugees</u>

\#

Dmitry wanted to impress his Kremlin bosses, he and the other Russian soldiers gave the Palestinian refugees rifles. They then were escorted to a fire range area where they'd practice.

\#

"Alright, since you were all rejected by the Oasis Defense, you will be on the front lines for Russia's war against NATO and her allies!" roared Dmitry.

\#

A few of the Palestinians really didn't want to be there, it was understandable with their situation. But Dmitry didn't seem to care, he encouraged them to fire at the tree barks for practice. BANG, BANG, BANG went the rifles as the Palestinian refugees fired a few rounds.

\#

"Good, good keep it up this will be good practice before moving onto the Finnish border" continued Dmitry.

\#

Dmitry continued to observe the Palestinian refugees for the next several hours; meanwhile in Lenin's tent, Lenin decided to trek towards the training area to check up on his brother. Dmitry could see that his brother hardly was at work training the lone Palestinian.

\#

"Why are you not training him in firearms?!" yelled Dmitry.

\#

Dmitry was being rather strict with his brother, but he needed to show it.

\#

<u>Lenin's Explanation</u>

\#

Lenin knew Salem was just tired and needed some rest from such a long journey. He could tell that the men and women involved in the Palestinian side were also in a similar shape.

\#

"Brother, you are overworking the refugees" said Lenin, "the refugee that's with me is tired."

\#

Dmitry laughed, he couldn't believe how weak his brother was.

\#

"Tired, tired?!" cried Dmitry, "War never takes a nap brother! You get that Palestinian up and bring him right to the firearms practice now!"

\#

Dmitry was being forceful with Lenin, he could see that Lenin was being too compassionate to the refugees. Lenin had no choice as he headed back towards his tent, there Salem was still fast asleep. Lenin had to tug on Salem a few times trying to get him to wake up.

\#

"Sorry to bother you" said Lenin as Salem finally woke up, "but you are required to take a firearms training."

\#

Salem froze - firearms training? He failed that sort of basic training with the Oasis Defense. Not even being able to hold a gun property resulted him in being disqualified to be involved in one of their many factions against the Israeli government.

\#

<u>Frighten Salem</u>

\#

Salem knew he had to face this alone as he got up from his slumber.

\#

"Alright, I will go to the firearms training" sighed Salem.

\#

Lenin could tell there was something the matter with his Palestinian counterpart as he led him towards the firearms training. But once Salem arrived, he could see the other refugees were also tired from the shooting range.

\#

"Look, everyone's tired why are you allowing this?" asked Salem.

\#

Lenin couldn't reply knowing his brother Dmitry would be unhappy. Soon Dmitry appeared and noticed Salem.

\#

"You, pick up a gun and start firing at the tree barks" continued Dmitry.

\#

Salem was having trauma issues with all of this. It was the Oasis Defense training all over again.

#

"I SAID PICK UP A WEAPON!" bellowed Dmitry.

#

Salem, frighten by Dmitry's outburst rushed to grab any weapon. He picked up a rifle and did his best trying to carry it. It was quite difficult for Salem. Dmitry sighed, he knew he had to only use a simple pistol to do the job.

#

"Lenin, fetch our Palestinian friend a pistol" sighed Dmitry.

#

Lenin complied and grabbed a pistol and exchanged the firearms with Salem.

Chapter Two

<u>Salem's Struggle</u>

#

Salem had never seen combat at all as he aimed his pistol carefully at a tree bark.

#

"When I say go, you will pull the trigger - GO!" ordered Dmitry.

#

BANG, BANG, Salem fired two shots. However one of the bullets somehow bounced off the tree bark and nearly missed one of the Russian soldiers just by a few inches.

#

"Hey, watch where you are aiming that gun!" bellowed the soldier.

#

Dmitry couldn't believe it, Salem was the weakest among the Palestinian refugees that the Oasis Defense had given them.

#

"It's no wonder why you are with us, you are a reject from their end!" bellowed Dmitry.

#

Tears began to pour out of Salem's eyes, he couldn't believe how cruel and sinister Dmitry was towards him. He simply soon drops the pistol and runs off. Lenin couldn't believe it either as he witnessed that.

#

"Salem, wait!" cried Lenin.

#

"Go fetch your coward of a friend" said Dmitry.

#

Dmitry grumbled knowing he had to deal with an incompetent Palestinian such as Salem. He just couldn't believe how incompetent he was. Salem ran past the camp just a few paces away from it just to try to escape.

#

Not Getting Far

\#

Salem couldn't get far from the camp as a few Russian soldiers were guarding the exit of the outpost.

\#

"Not so fast, no one leaves this area, no one" said one of the Russian soldiers.

\#

Soon Lenin comes into the scene trying to catch up with Salem.

\#

"Please don't run away!" cried Lenin.

\#

Lenin could see that Salem had a very challenging experience growing up in the West Bank. He could understand why Salem wasn't like the rest of the Palestinians at all.

\#

"Please, no more of this, find a way out for me, please I'm begging you!" cried Salem as he got on his knees.

\#

It was a dramatic moment for Salem, he couldn't pray to any higher power to help him. He was on his own trying to seek up, and he could only find it in the form of Lenin Aslanov.

\#

"I know you are frighten, but you must try to appease my brother" said Lenin.

\#

Lenin assured Salem to come back to the camp, hopefully Dmitry wouldn't punish Salem too harshly. Salem agreed and followed Lenin back to the camp. Dmitry smiled as he could see Lenin bringing Salem back.

\#

Punishing Salem for Cowardice

\#

Dmitry knew there were so many cowards on the battlefield of Ukraine fleeing, he didn't want Salem to give the other Palestinian refugees any ideas.

\#

"YOU, because you ran from me you will be forced to do various exercises and my brother will be the one to monitor your activities!" bellowed Dmitry.

\#

Dmitry was being serious and harsh with Salem. Dmitry gave a few orders here and there with various exercises and how many Salem should do. Ranging from push ups, sit-ups and even pull-ups. He was going to do at least a hundred each.

\#

"You are to do a hundred of these exercises and Lenin will keep watch of you doing them, do I make myself clear?" asked Dmitry.

\#

"Yes sir" sighed Salem.

\#

"GET GOING!" bellowed Dmitry.

\#

Salem started with the push-ups since they were the easiest. Lenin began to count to make sure he was going to go up to a hundred. Salem was already getting tired when he was reaching the half-way mark. Lenin kept on counting, trying to encourage Salem to finish the exercise.

\#

"Just keep on trying" said Lenin.

\#

Salem did his best with the push-ups and managed to finish.

\#

<u>Continuing With the Other Exercises</u>

\#

Salem continued with the sit-ups as the next set of exercises. Lenin had to assist by grabbing his shoes so that Salem could do them.

\#

"Yes, that's right just keep it up" said Lenin.

#

Lenin was encouraging Salem to complete the exercises just as he did with the push-ups. Dmitry chuckled knowing that his brother was useful after all. He headed off to his tent to report on the training of the Palestinian refugees. Once he arrived in his tent he soon turned on a walkie talkie to speak to his supervisor.

#

"Everything is going according to plan, the refugees are getting use to their firearms training" said Dmitry.

#

"Excellent, any issues with any of the refugees?" asked the supervisor on the other end.

#

"There is one troublesome refugee that was too much of a coward with using a mere firearm" continued Dmitry, "he was frighten just firing a pistol!"

#

"Really?" laughed the supervisor, "Keep a close eye on this one. He might try to influence your brother's pacifist nature not to fight the Finns."

#

Dmitry knew that Salem could become a problem for him, he would have to keep a closer eye on him.

Chapter Three

<u>Trouble for Salem</u>

#

The exercise punishments went smoothly for Salem, with Lenin keeping a watchful eye on him. Lenin was doing his best trying to encourage Salem to pull through. It was when Salem had to do pull-ups, the choice that Dmitry had in mind was a very cold metal bar that was raised over a tower. When Salem grabbed on, it was quite cold.

#

"It's so cold!" cried Salem.

#

"Come on, I know you can do it" said Lenin.

#

Lenin could see Dmitry was watching them from afar. Dmitry could tell his brother Lenin could become a problem for him and the Palestinian refugees involved in his incursion scheme.

#

"That brother of mine is going to ruin everything!" thought Dmitry in his head.

#

Dmitry could tell that his brother Lenin was being too compassionate to someone like Salem. Salem was the weakest link among the Palestinian rejects from the Oasis Defense. He could get the feeling why Salem was an outcast among his own kind. Not willing to fight, and unwilling to follow orders.

#

"Please try to make it" said Lenin.

#

Lenin could see that Salem was struggling because of how cold the metal was.

#

<u>Salem Slips!</u>

#

Salem got to nearly 20 pull-ups as he was on the cold metal bar, trying to bring his chin up towards the bar itself. It was so cold and slippery!

#

"I am losing my grip!" cried Salem.

#

"Please keep on trying, you don't want to get my brother mad!" cried Lenin.

#

Dmitry chuckled at this from afar.

#

"You are right that I will be mad" laughed Dmitry in his head.

#

Dmitry enjoyed seeing others toil in their misery, Salem was doing his best trying to hang onto the very cold metal bar. It was when he began to notice he was slipping from it! He was already a bit high trying to do the pull-ups.

#

"I'm falling!" cried Salem.

#

"Please, don't give up!" cried Lenin.

#

Salem couldn't help himself, the cold metal bar couldn't keep him still. He couldn't continue doing the pull-ups anymore. Soon he slipped and fell right into the snow itself. FLOP! Salem managed to pick himself up, Dmitry soon walked over and took a look at Salem.

#

"I COUNTED TWENTY!" bellowed Dmitry, "YOU SHOULD HAVE DONE A HUNDRED TO MAKE UP FOR YOUR COWARDICE!"

#

A tear trickled down Salem's eyes, he knew he couldn't take the pressure.

#

<u>Lenin Defends Salem</u>

#

Lenin had enough of his brother's ruthless behavior not just towards Salem, but to the other Palestinians. Though none of them were as cowardly as Salem was, it was all the same. They were inexperience fighters, and Dmitry wanted the incursion to go well.

#

"ENOUGH!" bellowed Lenin as he stood in between the two men.

#

Dmitry laughed as he could see his brother was the weak link.

#

"You want to defend them so much, I will be assigning you to lead them during the incursion of the Finnish border!" laughed Dmitry.

#

Lenin gasped, he couldn't believe he was going to lead an incursion! He had never done such a thing before!

#

"But, I never led a group, I have done missions on my own but not with a group" said Lenin.

#

"Well, there's a first time for everything brother, and since you are such a fond defender of him, he can be your right-hand man" laughed Dmitry.

#

Dmitry knew selecting a coward like Salem as Lenin's partner would surely get his brother in trouble should he be caught by the Finns. Dmitry laughed as he continued to head off.

#

<u>Salem Thanks Lenin</u>

#

Salem gazed at Lenin, no one has ever come to his defense like that.

#

"Thank you" said Salem as he gave Lenin a friendly hug, "no one has ever done that for me in my entire life!"

#

"What happened back in the West Bank with your training?" asked Lenin.

#

"Well, they wanted me to fight against the Israelis and their Temple Movement" continued Salem, "I am not a fighter, I'm against this senseless war."

#

"I am having second thoughts about this too" added Lenin.

#

Lenin and Salem decided to walk back towards Lenin's tent. Lenin could tell that his brother Dmitry was planning to promote the incursion soon.

#

"Your brother seems like he will be doing anything to help his bosses in the Kremlin" said Salem.

#

"Yes" replied Lenin, "my brother can be quite ruthless. He doesn't seem to care one shred of human dignity inside of him."

#

Lenin then made a campfire near his tent and Salem sat down to warm himself up. Meanwhile for Dmitry he was documenting Salem's most recent failures to his supervisors back in the FSB. He knew they wouldn't be pleased, but felt progress was still being made.

Part Two

Chapter Four

<u>Alerting the Bosses</u>

\#

Dmitry called in his supervisor through his communicator device within his tent.

\#

"Yes Dmitry, have you finished training the Palestinian fighters yet?" asked the supervisor.

\#

"Well, there is one troublesome fighter known as Salem Barid, he's a coward!" bellowed Dmitry.

\#

The supervisor paused on the other end.

\#

"Yes, that could complicate matters, the Finns could immediately see it as well" added the supervisor, "who have you assigned Salem to?"

\#

"My brother Lenin" continued Dmitry, "Lenin is too compassionate towards him and the other Palestinians."

\#

"The Palestinian rejects are mere canon fodder to us" laughed the supervisor, "they will make good headlines for the international news to be used against the West."

\#

Dmitry and his bosses in the Kremlin had a sinister plan for the country of Finland - depict Finland as a "genocidal" Western country by using Palestinian fighters as canon fodder! It would be a stroke of propaganda victory for the Kremlin should everything move forward. Meanwhile, for the Palestinian refugees themselves, the Russian soldiers were increasingly becoming wary of their situation.

\#

"I do not think they will be helping us that much" remarked one Russian soldier as he and a few of the soldiers were on patrol around the tents.

\#

"They all look like they're home sick" added another soldier.

#

The soldiers knew there could be some resistance to the mission ahead.

#

<u>Ready for the Incursion</u>

#

As morning soon rose for the next day, it was finally time for the incursion to begin. Palestinian rejects of the Oasis Defense rose up from their tents. They lined up where the Russian soldiers of the Iron Curtain Security had instructed them to stand.

#

"That's it, keep moving" said one soldier.

#

"I want to go home" said a Palestinian man.

#

"You are doing this for the glory of the Kremlin!" bellowed another soldier.

#

But it seemed like from the mood of the Palestinians themselves, they didn't want to be here at all. They had no choice, no other options were left for them. Soon it was morning for Salem and Lenin. Salem got out of the tent and stretched, he then noticed soldiers were heading towards a certain area of the camp.

#

"What's going on?" asked Salem.

#

"The incursion, it must be today!" cried Lenin as he got up.

#

Lenin and Salem headed over towards the designated area, Dmitry was there waiting for them.

#

"YOU TWO ARE LATE!" bellowed Dmitry.

\#

Dmitry wasn't pleased to see that his brother had too much compassion for Salem. That needed to change soon.

\#

<u>Giving Everyone Rifles</u>

\#

The Palestinians standing before Dmitry were soon handed rifles by various soldiers. Salem was given a rifle along with Lenin.

\#

"You two will be leading the incursion" continued Dmitry, "you are to trek over to the Finnish border and incite the Finns to attack you."

\#

"But isn't that aggression?" asked Salem.

\#

Dmitry heads over to Salem and slaps him right in the face.

\#

"Don't you dare question the motives of this mission!" bellowed Dmitry.

\#

Salem couldn't believe he had been snapped as he felt his face, Lenin couldn't say a word in opposition knowing his brother would do the same to him.

\#

"I will have no further questions about this mission, do I make myself very clear?" asked Dmitry.

\#

The majority of the Palestinians nodded in agreement.

\#

"Very good, you are to march out, my brother Lenin has done a few scouting missions to the Finnish border, shouldn't be too hard to figure out from there" continued Dmitry, "MOVE, MOVE!"

\#

Lenin and Salem began to march together in the snow with the Palestinian rejects following them behind. The armed Palestinian men and women were quite frighten to what might happen next.

#

The Finnish Border

#

The march from the Iron Curtain Security camp to the Finnish border took at least thirty minutes in the snow. It was especially rough for them all since they didn't travel by any sort of vehicle.

#

"I can't believe we're doing this on foot" remarked a Palestinian man.

#

"Well, I heard from one of the soldiers, it's because the Finns would spot us if we use a vehicle" added a Palestinian woman.

#

The Palestinian man rolled his eyes, he and the others never had to do this sort of extensive training when they were in the West Bank. Lenin halted the rest of the group as they were approaching the Finnish border. The Finns had laid out a long stretch of barred wire across their border to prevent any further intrusion. Lenin didn't know if the Finns laid any mines in the process.

#

"Let's just make sure there are no traps at all" said Lenin.

#

Lenin carefully approached the barred wire, surely enough there were no mines around the barred wire at all. It was safe enough for everyone to get through, meanwhile up on a guard tower not far a Finnish border guard could see a few intruders below with his binoculars.

#

Finns Alerted!

#

The Finnish soldier could see a few Palestinian refugees trying to dig their way underneath the barred wire that was there. He couldn't believe it, what were Palestinians doing near the border of Finland?

#

"Better send in the silent alarm" said the Finnish soldier.

#

The soldier soon pressed the silent alarm button on his tower, surely enough Finnish soldiers in snow gear began to mobilize, they headed out on their snowmobiles closer and closer towards the commotion. They could see little dots in the snow as they were approaching.

#

"Halt, stop!" cried one of the soldiers as he parked the snowmobile and got out.

#

The lone Finnish soldier led the charge against those who were behind the incursion. Little did the Finnish soldiers realize, they were falling for the Kremlin's plan to cause an international crisis! A Palestinian man opened fired on the lone Finnish soldier injuring him in the leg.

#

"Take cover!" cried the soldier.

#

Other Finnish soldiers soon joined in, using the snow as their cover. Their white suits made it difficult for Lenin and Salem to see where they were coming as the bullets began to rain down on them.

Chapter Five

<u>Firing Back</u>

#

The Palestinian rejects of the Oasis Defense did their best to fire upon the Finnish soldiers. The snow made it more difficult for them to see their every movement.

#

"I can't see any of them!" cried a Palestinian man as he tired to aim his rifle.

#

Some of the Oasis Palestinian fighters were just shooting bullets at the snow, even Salem nearly did the same thing when he aimed his rifle. But Lenin could see the movement of the Finnish border soldiers getting closer.

#

"They're coming right at us!" cried Lenin.

#

BANG, BANG, a Finnish soldier fired his gun which sent one of the Palestinian men dropping to the snow. Another one soon followed, the Palestinian refugees kept on firing their rifles with Lenin and Salem leading the charge.

#

"We're actually doing it!" cried Salem.

#

Lenin couldn't believe that his first major mission for Dmitry would be a success, despite his brother's ruthless behavior. It was a fierce fire fight between the two groups, but the Finns had the advantage. All they had to do was hold off until more reinforcements arrived.

#

"Keep on holding them back!" cried one of the Finnish soldiers.

#

The Finns knew something strange was going on, why on Earth was the Russian government using Palestinian refugees to do their dirty work?

#

Incursion Battle

\#

The fierce fighting continued in the snow, with more on the Palestinian side dropping dead due. The Finnish soldiers were moving in quickly, Lenin and Salem could see they were losing so many people fast!

\#

"We have to get out, retreat!" cried Salem.

\#

"Wait, I didn't give the orders!" cried Lenin.

\#

Salem ignored Lenin's comments and soon ordered the rest of the Palestinian fighters to flee. Many of those who had survived with mostly women fighters with a few men tagging along. The ones who were not so lucky laid in the snow, Lenin knew he had to join Salem while fleeing. Lenin fired his rifle at the Finnish soldiers as he ran backwards helping to provide cover for Salem and the others. Lenin was no doubt disappointed with Salem's cowardly behavior, his brother Dmitry had a point.

\#

"What are you doing giving them such an order, you know my brother already doesn't trust you" said Lenin.

\#

Salem knew he screwed up as they took cover from the Finnish soldiers.

\#

"I'm so sorry, it's just there were too many soldiers on the other end!" cried Salem.

\#

Lenin rolled his eyes, he wondered if this was the reason why Salem was rejected by the Oasis Defenders.

\#

Pinned Down

\#

Finnish soldiers marched over the bodies of the fallen, they could get some sense they were looking for the two who were leading the incursion.

\#

"They have to be close by" said a Finnish soldier, "spread out and search!"

#

The Finns were having none of it, they were determine to make sure that whoever was leading the incursion would be caught and prosecuted. Lenin and Salem could see they were getting closer and closer towards their position.

#

"This is crazy, you told everyone to run and leaving us alone!" cried Lenin.

#

"I wasn't thinking, I'm sorry!" cried Salem.

#

Lenin knew he had to find a way to distract the Finns, he knew only a mere snowballs would have to do.

#

"I have an idea" said Lenin, "but it'd take teamwork to do it."

#

Salem nodded and listened on Lenin's plan, the Finnish soldiers were coming closer and closer to their position. One of the Finnish soldiers spotted what seemed like the traditional Russian hat.

#

"Freeze!" ordered the Finnish soldier, "Put your hands up!"

#

The hat laid motionless, as the Finnish soldier approached the hat it was just simply on top of a mount of snow. Then a snowball came hurling right at him.

#

<u>Distracting the Finnish Soldiers</u>

#

The lone Finnish soldier couldn't believe who hit him with a mere snowball. He gazed around trying to look for the perpetrator.

#

"Show yourself you coward!" bellowed the Finnish soldier.

\#

Other Finnish soldiers began to also get pelted by snowballs as well. Lenin and Salem were doing their best trying to distract them.

\#

"We have to keep at it!" cried Lenin.

\#

Salem didn't know how long this would last, he knew he just had to survive. As for the other Palestinian members of the Oasis Defenders, they arrived back at the Iron Curtain Security camp. Dmitry was flabbergasted that so many fighters were still alive.

\#

"YOU ARE ALL COWARDS, WHERE ARE SALEM AND LENIN?!" cried Dmitry.

\#

"I think they were left back at the Finnish border" remarked a Palestinian woman.

\#

Dmitry rolled his eyes, he couldn't believe how incompetent his brother Lenin was.

\#

"YOU IDIOTS LEFT HIM TO BE CAPTURED BY THE FINNS?!" cried Dmitry.

\#

Dmitry's yelling at the Oasis Defenders was more ruthless than their own overseers who were training them. Dmitry couldn't believe it, if Lenin gets captured his job would surely be on the line.

\#

A Lucky Break

\#

Back at the Finnish border, the Finnish soldiers were distracted enough by the snowball barrage against them that Lenin and Salem had to make a run for it. Lenin knew he would be punished by his brother Dmitry, but he'd have to worry about that when he arrived at the camp.

\#

"They're too busy!" laughed Lenin.

\#

Lenin was happy his plan worked out quite nicely as he could see the confused Finnish soldiers in the distance. Salem still felt sorry for giving the marching orders for his fellow Palestinians to flee when so many of them fell.

\#

"Please, allow me to take the full blame for the failure" said Salem, "I gave the marching orders to flee ignoring your commands."

\#

Lenin sighed.

\#

"Fine" said Lenin, "I will make sure Dmitry will not punish you too harshly."

\#

The two continued their trek back to the Iron Curtain Security camp, it took them nearly at least an hour in the snow to get there. By the time arrived, Dmitry was waiting for them at the entrance with at least a dozen Russian soldiers. He did not look too happy at all.

Chapter Six

<u>Angry Dmitry</u>

#

Dmitry was ticked off by his brother Lenin for letting so many Palestinians flee the incursion fight. Lenin did his best trying to explain it wasn't his orders, but Dmitry was having none of it.

#

"I do not care who's fault it is" said Dmitry, "in fact, I am prepared to punish you BOTH since I did assign both of you to the mission."

#

Lenin and Salem both gasped, Dmitry was right, Dmitry did assign both of them.

#

"W-W-What are you going to do to us brother?" asked Lenin.

#

"I don't know, I will have to think of something quite painful" laughed Dmitry, "I will have to see what the entire global media states on your failure first."

#

Dmitry heads over to his tent as the Russian soldiers stand guard over Lenin and Salem. Both of them knew they were in big trouble because of their cowardly and incompetent behavior. As Dmitry strolled towards his tent, he soon turned on the radio.

#

"Reports at the Finnish border with Russia have reported a possible incursion from what appeared to be Palestinian refugees" said a male reporter on the radio, "for some strange reason Palestinians were used."

#

Dmitry smiled as he continued to listen to the report.

#

<u>Odd Finnish Incursion</u>

#

The radio report continued with Dmitry listening in on every word.

#

"The Finnish government officials were perplexed to find Palestinians on the border sharing Russia" continued the male reporter over the radio, "they didn't have the slightest clue how they got there."

#

"We are carefully examining and investigating this as we more details come in from the Finnish soldiers that fought the incursion at the border" said an male Finnish official, "we are unsure how these Palestinians got there or who sent them there."

#

"Why did they have rifles with them as what it states with the report?" asked the male reporter.

#

"Someone must have trained them to try to cause an incident like this" said the male Finnish official, "we do not know who is behind it, but we can be certain it's the hallmarks of the Kremlin trying to insight an international crisis."

#

Dmitry could see that the strategy was working trying to confuse the Finnish government. He soon turned off the radio and soon headed back to where Lenin and Salem were being watched by the Russian soldiers. Dmitry was quite happy with the sort of progress the incursion incited.

#

Dmitry's Punishment

#

Dmitry was in a happy mood, but he still had to punish his brother Lenin for his incompetent behavior and Salem for his cowardice.

#

"I still do not like either of you" said Dmitry, "but the only good news is the incursion was a success. It was a propaganda victory for the Kremlin."

#

"Does that mean we do not get to be punished?" asked Salem.

#

"No, in fact, I have decided to give you two an assignment" continued Dmitry, "you are to use a pick ax to carve an ice sculpture of me in my honor so I can show my bosses in the Kremlin of my great achievement!"

\#

Lenin and Salem sighed with a relief - an ice sculpture of Dmitry, that shouldn't be too hard right?

\#

"You two will share the punishment, lucky for both of you I already found a large enough ice block for both of you to work on" continued Dmitry.

\#

Dmitry then encouraged the Russian soldiers to escort Salem and Lenin to another disclosed part of the camp. This part of the camp was more of Dmitry's private area where he got to relax and have more leisure time for himself.

\#

Dmitry's Arrogance

\#

Lenin never saw this side of his brother as he gazed around this portion of the camp. Dmitry was an art collector of some sort, and on occasion would spend some free time creating various pieces of art.

\#

"I never was able to master ice sculpting" said Dmitry, "but I figured it would be a good punishment to get you two to have my likeness in it."

\#

Salem and Lenin both swallowed as they could see a rather large ice block was there.

\#

"You have at least until the end of the week to sculpt an ice statue of myself" said Dmitry, "fail to do it and I will upgrade the punishment!"

\#

Dmitry was serious as he handed Salem and Lenin the pick axes, both of them were given a portrait of Dmitry that they could use as a guide.

\#

"This will take some effort" sighed Lenin.

#

Lenin could see why his brother Dmitry was always so rude and arrogant, this was the reason why. Salem couldn't believe how large the ice block was.

#

"This will take us forever!" cried Salem.

#

"If we start now, we can show my brother what we're both made of" said Lenin.

#

Lenin encouraged Salem to help with the project, much to Salem's reluctance.

Chapter Seven

<u>The Ice Sculpture Punishment</u>

\#

Salem still couldn't believe what a large block of ice he had to pick through using the pick ax. He began to copy Lenin, as Lenin began to apply the pick ax in certain areas where he could create the image of his brother Dmitry.

\#

"Just like this" said Lenin.

\#

Lenin was doing his best trying to show Salem it wasn't that hard at all. Salem did his best by raising the pick ax in one area of the ice cube and began to get to work. The Russian soldiers observed both of them from afar, they could see they had quite a bit of work to cut out for them.

\#

"Looks like they're moving forward, probably will take them at least a few days" said one of the soldiers.

\#

Lenin knew he had to find a way to escape the camp, he got some sense that Salem wasn't happy at all.

\#

"There must be a way we can get out of this" said Salem.

\#

"I think it'd take me sometime to figure out where we can flee" said Lenin, "there is no area that's safe unless."

\#

"Unless what?" asked Salem.

\#

Lenin though of Vyborg which would be the closet Russian city near the Finnish border as a possible escape route.

\#

<u>Thinking of Escaping</u>

\#

After nearly a day on the ice sculpture, the soldiers escorted both Salem and Lenin back to Lenin's tent. Dmitry decided to inspect the ice cube that was being used to carve an ice sculpture out.

#

"Not, bad, not bad" said Dmitry as he checked up on the ice sculpture.

#

He then headed over towards his brother's tent where Lenin and Salem were both trying to rest.

#

"I must say brother" said Dmitry as Lenin came out, "you and Salem are quite the team."

#

"So does that mean you'll not punish us further?" asked Lenin.

#

"Let's not get too carried away, I will make sure the soldiers will keep watch on the both of you" said Dmitry.

#

Dmitry soon headed off, Lenin knew it would be hard for him and Salem to make a run for it now.

#

"Well, did Dmitry agree not to punish us further?" asked Salem.

#

"No" replied Lenin, "we have to figure a way out of this camp, but there are too many guards."

#

Salem knew he had to get some of his fellow Palestinians to stir some sort of uprising if they ever wanted to get out.

#

<u>Salem's Plan</u>

#

When morning soon came, both Lenin and Salem soon got out of the tent to stretch. The soldiers soon gave them a small meal and escorted them towards where the ice cube was located.

#

"Boss still wants you both to work on the ice sculpture" said one of the soldiers.

\#

Salem knew he had to find some free time to get to his Palestinian counterparts. As the two continued to work, Lenin wanted to cover for Salem to take a break from picking the ice cube. The Russian soldiers who were stationed there to watch them allowed Salem to take the break.

\#

"I see no harm in that" said one of the Russian soldiers.

\#

Salem was able to have at least fifteen minutes of a break from sculpting the ice sculpture, plenty of them to head off to meet up with his fellow Palestinians. Once he arrived he could still see that his own people were still suffering from the losses of the incursion they caused at the Finnish border. It was no life for them at all to be stranded here like this.

\#

"So depressing" thought Salem as he gazed around.

\#

Salem knew it would be tough for him to crack the Oasis Defense rejects to helping him stir some sort of distraction.

\#

<u>Unhappy Refugees</u>

\#

Salem could see that his fellow Palestinians were still quite unhappy where they are. He needed to provide them with words of encouragement.

\#

"Fellow Palestinians, I can see you all do not like it being in Russia" said Salem.

\#

Both the men and the women all nodded in agreement.

\#

"I lost my brother during that stupid incursion!" cried a Palestinian man.

\#

"I can't believe they made us do that!" cried a Palestinian woman.

#

It was far worse treatment that they had ever received, even far worse than when they were fighting the Israelis.

#

"Well fear not Palestinian brothers and sisters" continued Salem, "I have a plan, but I need your cooperation on trying to stop Dmitry."

#

The Palestinians all huddled together to listen in on Salem's plan.

#

"We need a diversion, enough people to cause a rebellionn in the camp itself" said Salem.

#

The Palestinian men and women continued to listen in on Salem's plan, it was a simple plan that'd certainly try to ruin Dmitry's reputation. They were purposely speaking the plan in Arabic which none of the Russian soldiers could understand as they began to observe them from afar.

Part Three

Chapter Eight

<u>Salem's Return</u>

#

Salem's break was soon over and soon he returned to where Lenin was still chipping away the ice from the ice cube with his pick ax.

#

"Well, do you have a plan of action?" asked Lenin.

#

"Yes" replied Salem, "I spoke to them in my native Arabic tongue. They know what to do in causing a distraction for us to escape."

#

"Great, just when will that plan happen?" asked Lenin.

#

"In a few hours" continued Salem, "the soldiers will probably have to check up on them every now and then before."

#

Salem continued to go back to work, working on Dmitry's ice sculpture. Meanwhile for the Palestinian refugees at the camp, the refugees knew they had to help Salem with his plan. They continued to go about their routine through out the camp. Ranging from doing their laundry for various members of the camp, to doing other chores. The Russian soldiers were unaware of any sentiment.

#

"We have to be careful around them" said a Palestinian man in Arabic to another man.

#

"Yes, I agree" added the second Palestinian man.

#

One of the men then decided to pretend to have a sprang ankle.

#

<u>Putting the Plan Into Motion</u>

#

Soon one of the Palestinian men held down his knee pretending to be in pain.

#

"MY KNEE, I THINK I BROKE IT!" cried one of the Palestinian men.

#

Soldiers began to rush over to check the lone Palestinian man out. Even the soldiers who were asked to watch over Lenin and Salem couldn't help but to wonder what was the commotion. It was just enough time to open a window of opportunity for the both of them to make a run for it.

#

"NOW, NOW!" cried Lenin.

#

Lenin and Salem ducked around a few crates in the camp hoping to not be seen by any member of the Iron Curtain Security group. The soldiers were too busy to focus on the lone Palestinian man. Then a Palestinian woman also cried out in pain pretending she was having a stomach issue.

#

"I think I might have eaten some bad food!" added a Palestinian woman.

#

Russian medics soon arrived on the scene of both incidents, Lenin and Salem knew they had a limited amount of time before the Russians realized the Palestinians were lying it.

#

"Come on, we have to find a vehicle and get out!" added Lenin.

#

Lenin and Salem continued to make their way throughout the camp, doing their best not to be spotted.

#

<u>Looking for an Escape</u>

#

Lenin and Salem managed to make it to the portion of the camp where they kept certain military vehicles. They didn't care what they stole, so long as they got out of the camp.

\#

"Which one do we choose?" asked Salem.

\#

Lenin did his best trying to think, there were so many vehicles to choose from that he didn't have time. Soon a lone Russian soldier spotted them.

\#

"Hey, what are you two doing here, neither of you are authorized!" cried the lone Russian soldier.

\#

Both Salem and Lenin lunged at the soldier and with a few punches here and there, the soldier was knocked out cold. Lucky for them, the soldier also had a key in his pocket for one of the vehicles.

\#

"Let's just choose one vehicle and get out of here" said Lenin.

\#

Lenin soon selected one of the vehicles, he and Salem soon got in and Lenin started the engine.

\#

"Move, move, I could hear more soldiers coming in!" cried Salem.

\#

The Russian soldiers noticed one of the vehicles was being taken.

\#

"STOP, STOP!" cried one of the Russian soldiers.

\#

BANG, BANG, the Russian soldiers fired warning shots, but Lenin soon took off.

\#

<u>Chasing Lenin and Salem</u>

\#

A few Russian soldiers got into a few vehicles and took off chasing them. Dmitry who was busy looking over some reports in his tent heard the commotion.

#

"Hey, what's going on?!" cried Dmitry.

#

Dmitry first went to check up on his brother Lenin at the ice cube area where the ice sculpture was going to be only to find them gone.

#

"THEY HAVE ESCAPED!" cried Dmitry.

#

Dmitry soon got out his walkie talkie and soon began to radio the soldiers.

#

"Mobilize all soldiers!" ordered Dmitry.

#

The soldiers did their best trying to comply, but the Palestinian refugees that they were around began to block their paths.

#

"Move, get out of the way!" ordered one of the soldiers.

#

"We will not let you harm one of our own!" remarked a Palestinian man.

#

The Palestinians were determine to stop the Russian soldiers, especially for how they were treated as pawns.

#

"We will be treated with respect" said a Palestinian woman.

#

The soldiers decided to draw their rifles, the refugees were not surprised by this. Dmitry noticed the commotion and stopped his own men from firing on them.

Chapter Nine

<u>Upset Dmitry</u>

#

Dmitry was clearly upset that his brother Lenin decided to escape with Salem. He could get the feeling that they were going to try to head to Vyborg. It was the Russian city closet to the Finnish border and a way for them to smuggle themselves into Finland.

#

"You are all in big trouble for helping my brother escape!" bellowed Dmitry.

#

"You are quite shameful for making us your pawns of your government" said a Palestinian woman.

#

Dmitry didn't care, the ice sculpture would have to continue.

#

"Guards, make the men continue my ice sculpture" said Dmitry.

#

"Yes sir" said one of the soldiers.

#

Dmitry then headed over to where the vehicles were located in the camp. He could already tell that most of the vehicles had been taken.

#

"I will have to catch up with my rebellious brother" thought Dmitry to himself.

#

Dmitry selected any vehicle, as he got into one, he soon headed off following the trail of vehicles. He could see the tracks in the snow quite clearly as he continued trying to catch up. Meanwhile, during the chase, Lenin and Salem were doing their best to dodge the oncoming bullets.

#

<u>Firing at the Escapees</u>

\#

BANG, BANG, BANG, shots continued to ring out as Lenin did his best trying to steer the vehicle during the chase. The snow made it much more difficult for him to steer.

\#

"They're still onto us!" cried Salem as he looked back.

\#

"I'm trying my best!" cried Lenin.

\#

Lenin couldn't believe that he didn't have a weapon on him to fire back, all he could do was try his best to dodge the bullets. BANG, BANG, BANG, more shots rang out as the Russian soldiers tried their best trying to pierce the tires of the vehicle they were driving.

\#

"I think my brother Dmitry is trying to catch up!" cried Lenin.

\#

Lenin could see his brother in the rear view mirror joining the other chase vehicles.

\#

"You should aim better!" roared Dmitry to the Russian soldiers.

\#

"We're trying!" cried one of the Russian soldiers.

\#

BANG, BANG, BANG, more shots rang out. Salem ducked, managing to dodge a few bullets that came his way. He couldn't believe how lucky he was when he managed to duck.

\#

"We're not going to make it!" cried Salem.

\#

Salem began to cry, he couldn't help it as it was in his nature.

\#

<u>Lenin's Words of Encouragement</u>

#

Lenin knew he had to be the voice of reason for Salem, he could see that Salem was crying in tears.

#

"You have to pull through this!" cried Lenin.

#

Salem still was crying he couldn't believe he was near death like this.

#

"It's just so dramatic!" cried Salem.

#

This was likely one of the reasons why he never made it past through basic training to be part of the Oasis Defenders. Such an individual like this wouldn't have made a great Palestinian fighter at all. Bullets still came raining down right and left, the Russian soldiers couldn't focus clearly as Lenin was steering the vehicle trying to dodge the bullets.

#

"Keep focus, focus on Vyborg!" thought Lenin in his head.

#

BANG, BANG, BANG, more bullets continued to be fired. Lenin could see one of the bullets managed to strike the rear view mirror knocking it right out of its foundation!

#

"That was a close one!" cried Salem.

#

"Pick up the mirror so I can see who is behind us" said Lenin.

#

Salem did his best and tried to bring up the mirror, he was so frighten on how the bullet managed to knock it right off.

#

<u>Cannot See Clearly</u>

#

Lenin couldn't see clearly as Salem was holding up the mirror that fell on the floor of the vehicle he was driving.

#

"Keep the mirror still!" ordered Lenin.

#

"I'm trying, I'm trying!" cried Salem.

#

Lenin continued to steer the vehicle, the steering made it difficult for Salem to hold up the mirror. The Russian soldiers could see the struggle between the two escapees.

#

"Looks like this will all be over very shortly" said one of the Russian soldiers.

#

"It better be!" laughed Dmitry.

#

Dmitry knew his brother Lenin wouldn't give up so easily, even if they were to be captured. Lenin could see he was just a few miles away from Vyborg, he continued to step on the gas of the vehicle to make it move forward.

#

"Come on, come on, almost there!" cried Lenin.

#

Dmitry laughed when he noticed Vyborg's city limits.

#

"They think they'll be safe in Vyborg?!" laughed Dmitry.

#

Dmitry didn't understand Lenin's strategy, however, Lenin wanted to find out the mysterious Black Bloc in the city. They were an extremist far left group known to help those who were dissatisfied with the Russian government.

Chapter Ten

Dmitry Pauses the Chase

#

Dmitry soon manages to catch up to the Russian soldiers who were doing their best trying to fire upon Lenin and Salem. He could see they'd always miss, every time they tried to take a shot. He signaled to halt and stop the chase for the time being.

#

"ENOUGH FIRING!" bellowed Dmitry.

#

The Russian soldiers soon halted their vehicles, they could tell their boss wasn't happy at all. He was rather disappointed that they allowed Lenin and Salem to pull off an escape from the Iron Curtain Security camp.

#

"Boss, they're going to get to Vyborg" said one of the Russian soldiers.

#

"Let them" continued Dmitry.

#

Dmitry knew the local FSB operatives who were operating in the city.

#

"But—" said one of the soldiers.

#

"Let them think they are safe" laughed Dmitry, "I know a few FSB operatives who are trying to search for the notorious Black Bloc members within the city. They have been a thorn for my bosses for sometime."

#

Dmitry soon got off the vehicle, he could see his brother and Salem were slowly drifting off in the horizon.

#

"So you want us to head back to the camp?" asked a soldier.

\#

"Yes, head back to the camp and make sure the other refugees don't start another rebellion" added Dmitry.

\#

The Russian soldiers soon sped off, for Dmitry he was going to go after his own brother by himself.

\#

<u>Arriving in Vyborg</u>

\#

Meanwhile, Lenin had never been to Vyborg before in his entire life, as for Salem, this was the first time he was in a major Russian city.

\#

"It's so beautiful" said Salem as he gazed around.

\#

"It really is" said Lenin, "we must find a place to hide so that my brother won't catch up."

\#

"You are certain he will try to find us?" asked Salem.

\#

"Knowing him, he will stop at nothing, if we can find the Black Bloc members within the city they'll surely help us find a way out of this" said Lenin.

\#

Lenin knew the safest route was to head to Western Europe and go from there. Despite being Russian himself, if he pretended to be a critic of the Russian regime the Western European nations would treat him with kindness. Lenin soon parks his vehicle in front of a bar with an anarchy symbol.

\#

"You are certain Black Bloc members could be here?" asked Salem.

\#

"It's worth a start" said Lenin as he got out of his vehicle.

\#

Salem still was so amazed by the city as he gazed around. He soon followed Lenin into the bar.

#

The Black Bloc Bar

#

Within the bar itself, a lonely bartender manned the front counter. Not much activity since it was still early in the morning when Lenin and Salem stepped in.

#

"What can I do for you two gentlemen?" asked the bartender.

#

"We're looking for the Black Bloc leader of the city" said Lenin.

#

The bartender froze, he gazed around just to make sure nobody else was around first.

#

"I am not supposed to tell you the address, but the leader of Vyborg's chapter - Sergei Romanov frequents this bar" continued the bartender, "he is often accompanied by his sister Capa" continued the bartender.

#

Lenin decided to stick around the bar along with Salem.

#

"We'll stay until they arrive" said Lenin.

#

"Okay, but you might be here for awhile, they normally don't come around until the late afternoon" continued the bartender.

#

Meanwhile in the outskirts of Vyborb, Dmitry was getting into his vehicle and heading into Vyborg itself. He knew his brother would be waiting around for the Black Bloc members to show up so he decided to try to trek towards the nearest FSB station. The local police station was always a front for the FSB much like their KGB counterparts during the Cold War used the regular police as their pawns.

#

<u>Vyborg's Police Station</u>

\#

Dmitry soon arrived at Vyborg's police station, knowing they were fellow FSB operatives who could assist in apprehending his brother and Salem he soon headed inside. The clerk at the front desk greeted Dmitry.

\#

"Can I assist you sir?" asked the clerk.

\#

"I need to speak with the police chief, I know his brother is an FSB operative" said Dmitry.

\#

The clerk paused and soon got up.

\#

"I will go fetch them" said the clerk.

\#

The clerk soon headed off and soon brought back Timur Sidorov and his brother Police Chief Viktor Sidorov. Timur immediately recognized Dmitry as a fellow FSB operative.

\#

"How goes the Finnish incursion scheme, I heard you had a few fallen refugees" laughed Timur.

\#

"Well, my brother has fled my camp and is in the city" continued Dmitry.

\#

"That is a problem" said Viktor, "we will deploy all the necessary resources to finding your brother and whoever is helping him."

\#

Dmitry had a strong sense that his brother was close by, but unsure where. As the hours passed to the late afternoon, back at the bar, Salem was getting quite bored just waiting around. He didn't have any drink because of his Islamic upbringing of no alcohol. Suddenly both Lenin and Salem could hear footsteps coming from the entrance of the bar.

Epilogue

<u>The Black Bloc Members</u>

#

Ms. Capa Romanov and her brother Sergei Romanov. A few masked men and women also entered the bar. They were Sergei's protection, the Black Bloc leader gazed at the two men at their usual seats at the bar.

#

"You two, move these are our usual seats" said Sergei, "you do not want to mess with the Black Bloc."

#

Lenin was happy to see the Black Bloc as he got up, Salem followed as they got up from their seats.

#

"Please, I am sorry for taking your seats but we came to search for you" said Lenin.

#

Sergei had a happy smirk on his face.

#

"For what reasons are you interested in the Black Bloc?" asked Sergei.

#

Salem soon got on his knees to Sergei.

#

"Please, I have come all the way from the West Bank, my friend Lenin assisted me in escaping an Iron Curtain Security camp" continued Salem, "we were used as canon fodder for an incursion into Finland."

#

Sergei who was against war could see where Salem was coming from.

#

"Just where would you like to flee?" asked Sergei.

#

Salem couldn't think of any place, but Sergei knew of one place that'd be the farthest away from the Kremlin's grasp - Iceland.

#

Sergei's Tasks

#

Salem soon got up as he and Lenin soon were invited to join Sergei and Capa at the bar.

#

"We'll discuss our matters here" said Sergei, "I have a few tasks for both of you to complete before I am willing to do anything for you."

#

"Just what are those tasks in mind?" asked Lenin.

#

"The FSB has been a thorn in the Black Bloc even during their days as the KGB" continued Sergei, "I need you and your friend to blow up the police station."

#

Lenin froze, he had never done anything like that.

#

"Blow up a police station?" asked Lenin.

#

"Yes, the police stations are usually fronts for the FSB and other secret police members" continued Sergei, "ruining everything would make sure I will send you to a safe place."

#

"And where would that safe place be?" asked Salem.

#

"Iceland" continued Sergei, "we have a few members there who are willing to assist you. And with your help you can become full time members afterwards."

#

"We'll do it, my brother will surely flip when we destroy his FSB allies" laughed Lenin.

#

"My sister Capa will show you to our main headquarters in the city" said Sergei.

#

After having a few drinks with the Black Bloc members, Lenin and Salem soon began to follow them.

#

Following the Black Bloc

#

Lenin couldn't imagine the sort of extensive network that the Black Bloc had around Russia. He had heard about them during the Cold War when he was growing up, but never imagined they were so secretive.

#

"Are you sure this will bring us to freedom away from your brother?" asked Salem as they drove around the city following the Black Bloc members in their designated cars.

#

"I am certain, it will show my brother a thing or two what we can do" said Lenin, "he is likely using the FSB resources trying to find us."

#

Lenin knew he had to hurry following the Black Bloc members, he could get the sense that there were FSB operatives everywhere in the city! It would take sometime, but Lenin and Salem would surely have to get use to being involved with the Black Bloc. Would both of them succeed with the mission? Find out in the next exciting book!

* * *

Did you love *Arctic Shadows: A Lenin Aslanov Story Book 1: The Finnish Incursion*? Then you should read *Ivan Zhuk: Zhuk's Gambit Book 1 Mental Agony*[1] by Maxwell Hoffman!

[2]

Ivan Zhuk finds himself the center of unwanted attention, particularly Yuri Kozlov a Russian mobster and national who has shown distain for Ivan's Ukrainian background. But more importantly, Ivan's presence has the attention of Yuri's rival - Tamrat Hailu, an Ethiopian crime boss seeking to control Chicago's black gangs.

Read more at https://www.instagram.com/vader7800/.

---

1. https://books2read.com/u/mvpRdq

2. https://books2read.com/u/mvpRdq

About the Author

I graduated from California State University with a BA in History. I am fond of historical fiction, science fiction, fantasy, and horror.

Read more at https://www.instagram.com/vader7800/.

About the Publisher

I graduated from California State University of Northridge with a BA in History. I am fond of fantasy, science fiction, historical fiction and horror.

Read more at https://www.instagram.com/vader7800/.

9 798822 397652